Dedicated to all the parents who
power through challenging
bedtimes on minimal sleep.
You are all amazing!

JaidzM

The Bibalibet Goes to Bed

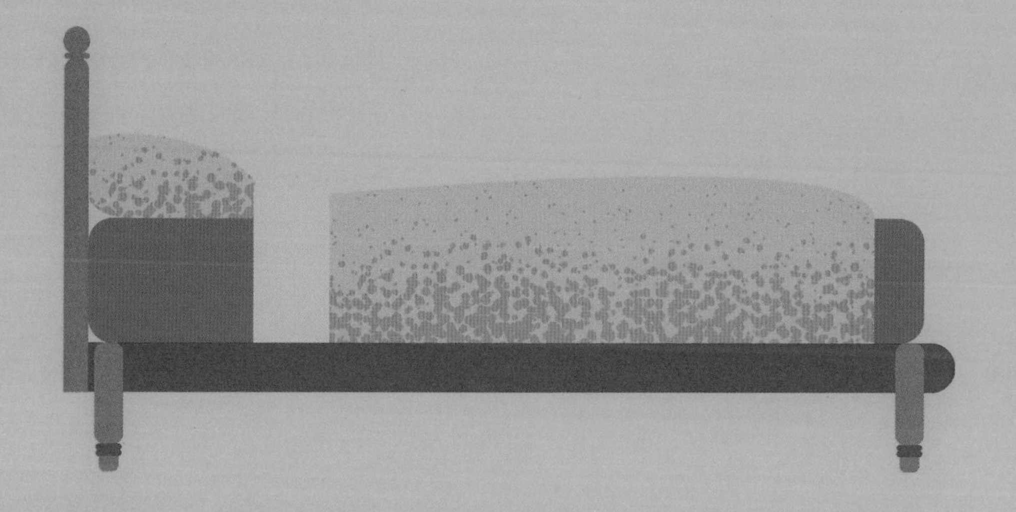

It had been a busy day for the Bibalibet.

He had spent the morning under the glare of the hot sun; darting between swimming in the sea and building sandcastles on the beach.

In the afternoon, he had raced around on the sandy shore for hours and hours, chasing after his rocket-shaped kite.

That evening, he treated himself to his favourite dinner of mashed potatoes and sausages, which was utterly satisfying.

Feeling worn out from all the fresh sea air and exercise, the Bibalibet stretched a great, big stretch and decided to get ready for bed.

The Bibalibet did the same
routine before bed every night.

First, he got in the bath, making
sure that there were plenty of
bubbles. He splished, sploshed
and splashed his way clean,
making a huge soggy mess on
the bathroom floor.

Then, he brushed his teeth and checked his smile, "Yep, still there." he said before climbing into his warm and snugly covers.

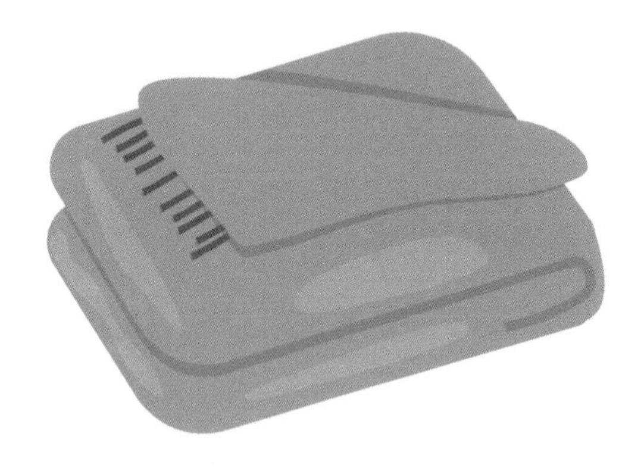

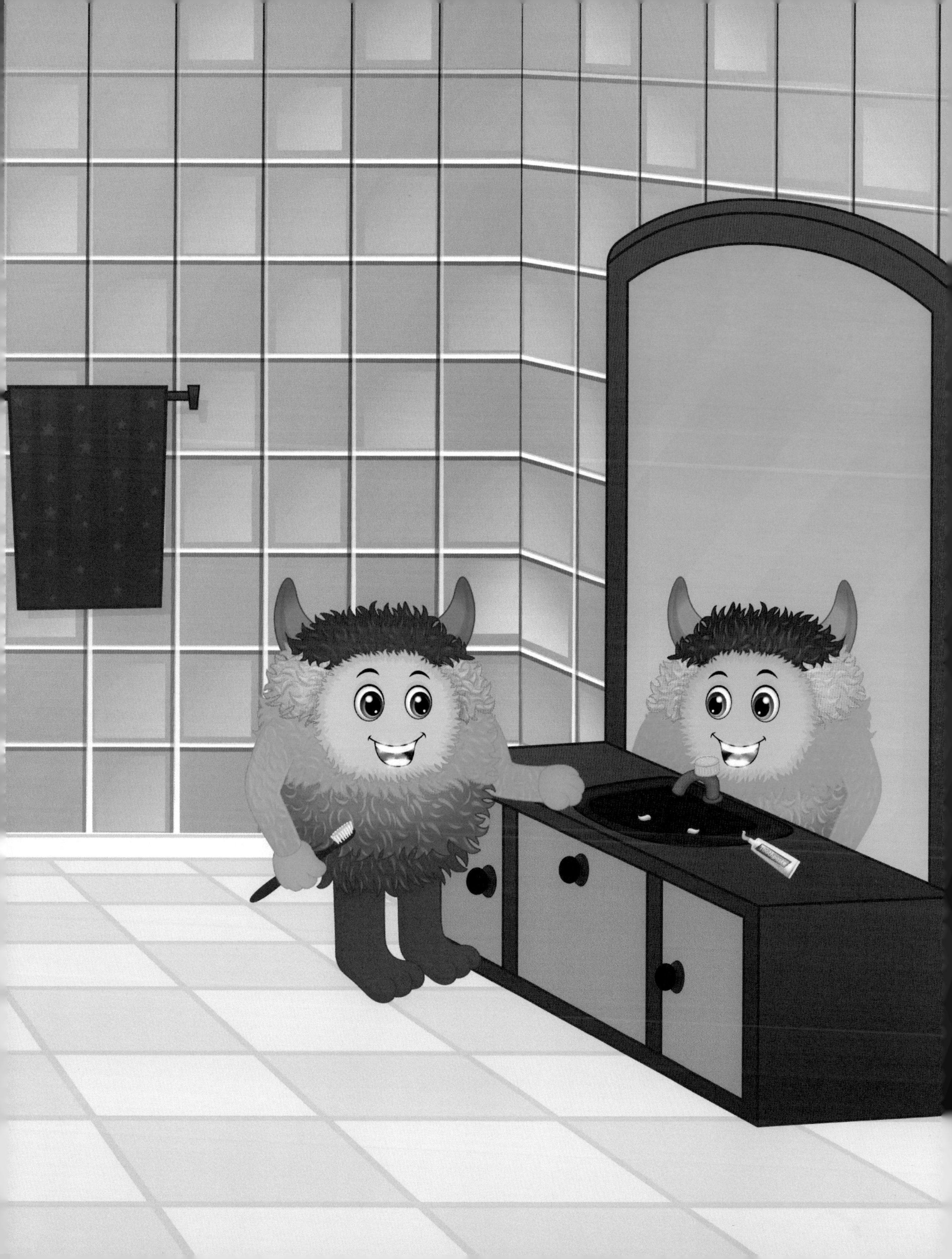

The sun had lowered its head, and it was time for the Bibalibet to go to bed.

Off went the light and just as our Bibalibet was closing his eyes, he heard a scratch, scratch, scratching from somewhere in the dark.

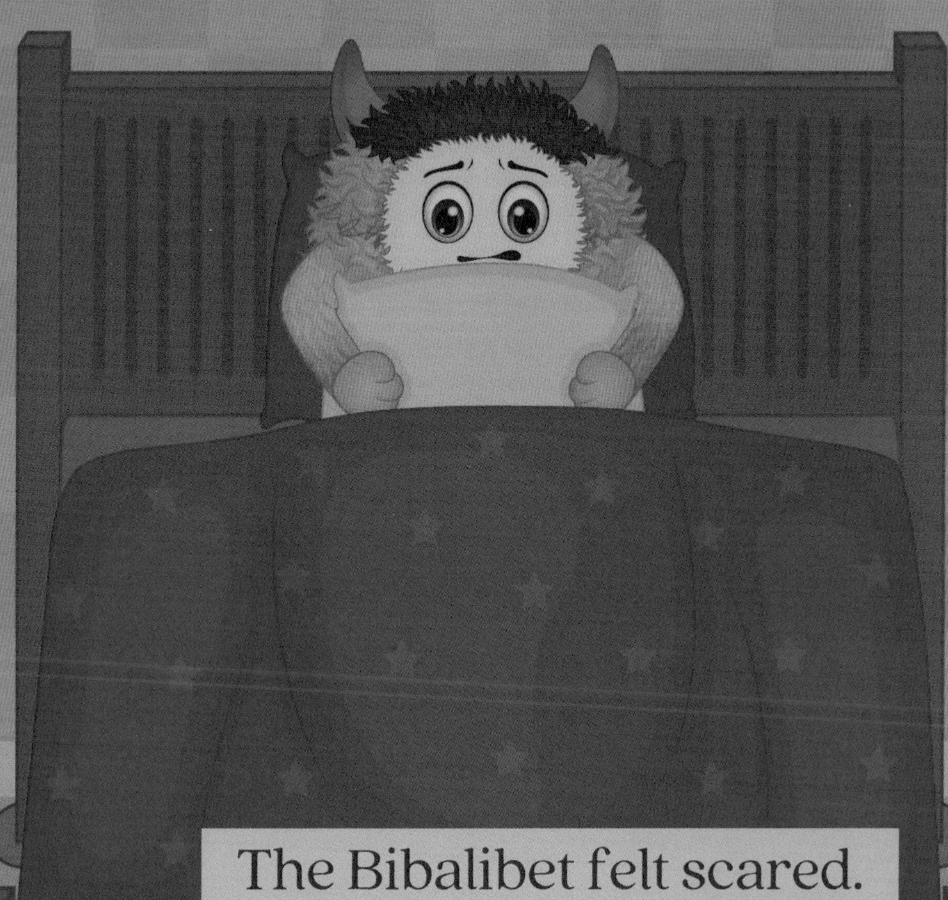

The Bibalibet felt scared.

“What was that noise?” he mumbled.

SCRATCH
SCRATCH
EEK
EEK

He had heard it again.

Too frightened to look, the Bibalibet delved deeper under the covers.

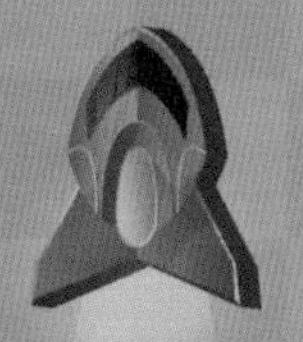

"I can't stay under here forever!" The Bibalibet thought to himself.

At that moment, he remembered what his mother had told him.

“If you ever feel scared, take a deep breath and count to 10.”

She had also said that things often seem scarier in the dark than they do in the light.

With that thought, the Bibalibet counted to 10.

"1, 2, 3, 4, 5, 6, 7, 8, 9, 10."

He flicked on his night lamp and decided to investigate.

1 2 3 4 5 6 7 8 9 10

He searched under his bed, in his cupboard, under his desk and even checked the window sill, but he didn't find anything.

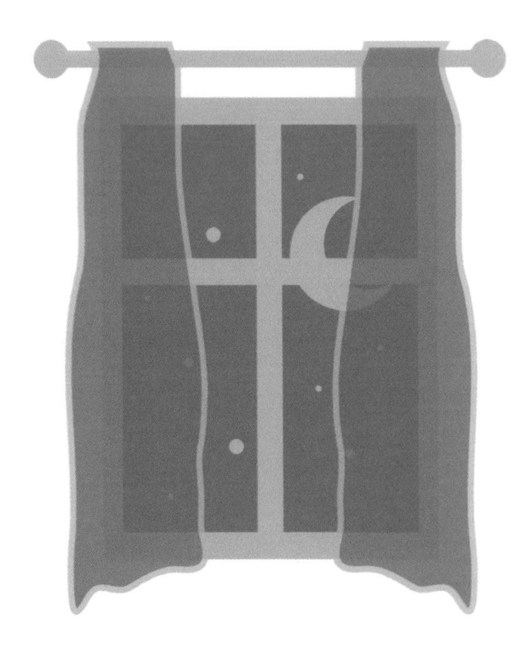

SCRATCH
SCRATCH
EEK
EEK

There it was again!

This time, the Bibalibet knew exactly where the sound was coming from.

He opened his bedroom door and on the floor was...

The cutest little mouse.

The mouse had wandered into the house through a hole in the wall, and she didn't know how to get back outside into the garden.

The Bibalibet scooped her up and took her to the garden, where her parents were waiting for her.

Daddy Mouse and Mummy Mouse were so pleased to see their baby.

They thanked the Bibalibet for his help.

Feeling pleased with himself for being so brave, the Bibalibet proudly wandered back to his room.

After all the excitement of the day, he felt exhausted.

The Bibalibet crawled back
into bed, turned off his night
light and went straight to sleep.

Sweet dreams Bibalibet.

Mindfulness Thoughts

FOLLOW
YOUR
DREAMS